AN AMISH COUNTRY TREASURE

RUTH PRICE

Copyright © 2015 Ruth Price

All rights reserved.

ISBN: 1517375851
ISBN-13: 978-1517375850

TABLE OF CONTENTS

ACKNOWLEDGMENTS	I
CHAPTER ONE	1
CHAPTER TWO	7
CHAPTER THREE	13
CHAPTER FOUR	23
CHAPTER FIVE	31
CHAPTER SIX	37
CHAPTER SEVEN	43
CHAPTER EIGHT	49
CHAPTER NINE	55
CHAPTER TEN	61
CHAPTER ELEVEN	69
CHAPTER TWELVE	75
CHAPTER THIRTEEN	81
CHAPTER FOURTEEN	87

AN AMISH COUNTRY TREASURE 2	93
CHAPTER ONE	94
CHAPTER TWO	101
CHAPTER THREE	109
CHAPTER FOUR	117
ABOUT THE AUTHOR	125

ACKNOWLEDGMENTS

All Praise first to the Almighty God who has given me this wonderful opportunity to share my words and stories with the world. Next, I have to thank my family, especially my husband Harold who supports me even when I am being extremely crabby. Further, I have to thank my wonderful friends and associates with Global Grafx Press who support me in every way as a writer. Lastly, I wouldn't be able to do any of this without you, my readers. I hold you in my heart and prayers and hope that you enjoy my books.

All the best and Blessings,

Ruth.

CHAPTER ONE

"Wait -- Jemima!"

Jemima King turned her head, but it was more out of habit than a real need to identify the voice. She would've known the sound of Mark Christner's voice in her sleep. They had lived next door to each other in the same Lancaster County community for 17 years.

He came running up and then stopped dead in the road. He bent double, caught his breath and laughed.

Jemima turned her eyes down demurely. Mark was always at her elbow these days. There was nothing new about that – they were childhood playmates – but Mark's reasons were different now.

She stole a glance at him through her lashes.

Mark was no longer the scruffy little boy of her childhood, and that was especially clear on a day like this one, when the sun gave his black hair a silky blue sheen, and made the curve of his cheek look as downy and smooth as a peach.

He was almost as tall as her father now. And his voice was nearly as deep. Jemima pinched in a smile. She would have to be made of stone not to notice that Mark had filled out nicely – especially when he flashed those beautiful white teeth in her direction.

She looked down at her feet. Their relationship was changing fast. The same Mark who had once irritated and teased her was – strangely -- becoming more solicitous by the day.

Maybe that was because *she* had changed, too.

Mark used to tease her about her red hair and green eyes. He had said she looked like an orange cat, and had made her cry.

But just the other day Mark had compared her hair to a maple leaf in the fall, and her eyes to the color of sunshine through leaves.

"I'll walk you home," he volunteered, and put a big brown hand out for her books.

Jemima smiled and gave them to him.

"What are you going to do, now that we've finished school? What are you going to do on *your* rumspringa, Mark?" she teased him. "Are you going to dress in English clothes and turn all the girls' heads?"

He grimaced wryly, and shook his head. "I'd just as soon dress up in a monkey suit," he said bluntly, and Jemima laughed outright.

"I'm disappointed in you, Mark," she said mischievously. "I was hoping you'd shock us all!"

Jemima enjoyed his chagrined expression out of her corner of her eye. She really shouldn't tease him, but it was *so* tempting. Mark was so *easy* to tease. No one she knew was more staunchly Amish, or more conservative. Mark reminded her of something big and strong and immovable, like the face of a mountain.

Or, maybe, *dormant volcano* would be a better description.

Because underneath all that unyielding rock, there was definitely warmth on the inside. She glanced at him affectionately then tilted her head, considering.

Maybe there was even a little *lava* under that mountain. She had seen one or two things lately that…

"Jemima, slow down!"

Jemima came back to herself. She stopped walking and turned around. Her little sister Deborah had fallen behind again, and was trotting along the dirt road to catch up.

"You… never… *wait for me*," Deborah complained, as she huffed along. She finally caught up with them and bent over double, gasping for breath.

Jemima looked at her little sister pityingly. Deborah's sandy brown hair had worked its way out from under her cap and was flying all around her face like a swarm of gnats.

She couldn't keep her hands from reaching out to smooth it back again. "Mind your hair, Deborah," she said softly.

Deborah swatted her hands away irritably. "I know how I look!" she snapped. "Maybe it's because I had to run! Next time just *wait* for me, and we can *both* look good!"

"That's no way to talk to your sis, Debby," Mark chided gently.

Deborah said nothing, but shot him a look that said, *Oh, shut up* as clearly as any words.

Jemima sighed and turned to him. "Never mind her, Mark, she has the temper of a wildcat. I know she doesn't mean half the things she says."

"I do, too – I mean *every word*!" Deborah countered, "Why shouldn't I, when you leave me behind to *flirt with your boyfriends*?"

"*Debby!*" cried Jemima and Mark, together.

"Oh, just forget it," Deborah fumed, "I'll walk home by myself. That's what you two *want*, anyway!" She hoisted her books up in her arms and stumped off, muttering under her breath.

Jemima shot Mark an apologetic look. "You'll have to forgive her, Mark," she explained, "Deborah's at that awkward stage. I'm sure that once it's over, she won't be – mad *all the time*."

Mark tilted his head and watched Deborah as she disappeared down the road. "I don't remember *you* ever being that –" He cleared his throat and quickly amended, "I mean, I don't remember that *you* ever had a… hard time."

Jemima shook her head. "She's driving poor Mamm to despair. It's only a few years until Debby comes of age, and the way she's treating all the boys she knows, not one of them is going to court with her!"

"Well, at least your Mamm will never have that problem with *you*." Mark looked at her with transparent admiration, and she blushed.

They rounded a corner and the King homestead gradually moved into view. It was a large, white, two story house surrounded by several outbuildings, including the blacksmith shop where Jemima's father worked. Even from that distance, the faint sound of a hammer rang out over the fields.

There was a buggy parked at the front of the house, and Mark's dark eyebrows moved together. He shaded his eyes with one hand.

"Whose buggy is that?" he frowned.

Jemima looked at him uncomfortably. "It's probably

Samuel Kauffman's," she murmured. "He said he'd be coming by this afternoon. His mother is sending Mamm some canning supplies."

Mark grunted suspiciously, and it was clear that he thought that Samuel Kauffman's mission was not primarily about preserving fruits and vegetables.

"Well, that sounds about right," he growled. "Samuel and your mamm are probably *trading recipes*."

"Mark!"

CHAPTER TWO

By the time they reached the front yard, it was clear that Samuel Kauffman was in attendance. His tall, slim frame was draped easily over one of the porch rails.

Samuel would have been at home at any beach in the world. He had a shock of bushy blond hair, he was brown as a nut, and his eyes were a sparkling blue. He greeted Jemima with a beautiful white smile and a wink that made her lower her eyes and go pink.

He acknowledged Mark with a cheery: "Well, look who's here! Sit down, Mark, you look exhausted. Can I get you a glass of water?"

Mark gave him a grim look, but replied: "I know you're *used* to doing that, but no thanks. We aren't at your folks' restaurant. Speaking of that – isn't it about time for you to put on your *apron*? It's getting close to dinner."

Jemima broke in hastily. "Samuel, it was very kind of you

to come all the way out here. I'm sure Mamm appreciates it."

Samuel beamed at her. "It's nothing, Jemima. Anytime! I'm always happy to do what I can."

"*That's for sure*," Mark mumbled under his breath.

Jemima's eyes moved uncertainly between the two of them. "Would the two of you like to – to stay to supper?" she ventured.

"Can't," Samuel lamented, and reached out to take her hand. "But give me a rain check, okay? I'd love to see you some *other* time."

Jemima noticed, with trepidation, that Mark's brow was gathering thunder, and he looked as if he was about to burst out with the accompanying lightning. So she hurried to reply, "Oh, I'm sorry you can't stay with us, Samuel. But yes, do drop by when you can," she smiled.

Samuel squeezed her hand and ran his thumb over her palm in a way that made it tingle. Then he smiled, bounded down the porch steps, and was driving away before she found the nerve to look up.

Mark watched him go with a scowl. "Why do you encourage that skinny little weasel?" he blurted.

Jemima went red. "Samuel is a very good person -- and you know it, Mark Christner!" she retorted indignantly. "I don't know *why* you take such a dislike to him, but he doesn't deserve it."

Mark turned to look at her, and his blue eyes were sad and reproachful. "Don't you, Jemima?" he asked softly.

Jemima couldn't meet his eyes, and felt her cheeks going hot. But she was spared the necessity of a reply by the sound of her father's heavy shoes approaching on the gravel drive. His booming voice cut off any possibility of a reply.

"Jemima, shouldn't you be helping your mamm with dinner?" he said pointedly, and directed a speaking look at Mark.

Mark's cheeks went a dull red. Jemima nodded, gave her visitor an apologetic look, and fled.

After she had gone, the six-foot-three Jacob King leaned against one of the porch posts and regarded his 17-year-old guest with a knowing look in his eye.

"How is your family, Mark?" he inquired gently.

"They're fine, sir," Mark mumbled.

Jacob nodded. "Good. I haven't seen much of them lately. Or of *you*, for that matter."

Mark looked out across the fields and bit his lip.

"And that's *not* good," Jacob sighed, running a massive hand through his rumpled red hair. "Because if a young man comes to this house to see my daughter, I expect him to come to see me *first*."

"Yes, sir."

"Just so long as we understand one another," Jacob smiled, and clapped his hand down on Mark's shoulder – hard.

Mark winced, but nodded.

Jacob smiled. "Staying to supper, boy?" he inquired gently.

"Ah – no. I have chores to do."

"Say hello to your folks for me," Jacob told him, and stood on the porch, watching, until Mark Christner's retreating form disappeared down the long dirt road.

Jacob King put both hands on his hips and laughed long and loud, and then turned and entered his house.

His wife Rachel was waiting for him at the door, with her arms crossed. "Jacob King, you should be ashamed of yourself," she chided gently. "Jemima is finished with her schooling now. It's *time* for her to be getting visits from young men. And Mark is her… *special friend*. He's plainly working up the nerve to ask if he can court with her. Why do you discourage him? Don't you *want* your daughter to find a good husband?"

Jacob leaned over and kissed his wife's pretty pink cheek. "You can set your mind at rest, Rachel," he assured her, "we'll never have to worry that Jemima will *lose* a man. Her danger is going to be picking the right one, out of the teeming horde!"

"Jacob, what a way to put it!" his wife exclaimed, but her lips curled up a little. "It's true that Jemima is *very* blessed, but how will she ever know which of her suitors is right for her, if she never gets a chance to spend time with them?"

Jacob sighed, and stretched his rippling arms. "Don't tire me with those silly pups, Rachel," he yawned. "I'm *hungry*. I've spent all day hammering over a forge, and I could eat a horse."

"Come to dinner then, Jacob," she smiled softly. "The table is laid."

Jacob's eyes lighted on a large cardboard box sitting on one of the dining room chairs. He lifted a canning jar.

"What's this?"

His wife assumed an innocent look, and shrugged. "Samuel Kauffman came by this afternoon to bring me some jars. It was a gift from his mother."

"Oh, *did* he now?"

Jacob met his wife's eyes, and raised his brows comically. She looked away, and pinched in a smile.

"Your dinner is getting cold."

Jacob sat down at the groaning dinner table, and rubbed his hands. But before his family bowed their heads to pray, he gave his pretty daughter a meaningful look.

"Jemima, the next time you see Samuel Kauffman, tell him *I'd like a word with him.*"

"Oh, Daed!" Jemima gave him a pleading look from her lovely eyes, but her father was the one male on earth who had found the strength to resist it.

"I mean it."

CHAPTER THREE

"You're so *lucky,* Mima," Ruth Yoder sighed. "I wish I had *your* problems."

The next afternoon, Jemima and her best friend were sitting in the woods just beyond the family garden, and were talking *boys*.

Jemima's friend rested her chin on her hands and raised impish blue eyes to the sky. "*Oh, Mark, stop it,*" she simpered. "*Samuel, you'll make me cry!*"

Jemima rolled her eyes. "If you say that again with a big scowl on your face, you'll sound almost like Debby," she sighed. "Does *everybody* hate me, then?"

Ruth giggled and relented. "Of course not, Mima. Everybody *loves* you. All the boys do, anyway, and the girls just wish they *were* you!"

Jemima eyed her friend ruefully. "I wish they didn't," she

confessed.

"Why not?" Ruth replied, stretching luxuriantly. She looked up at the sky through the tree branches. "If you've *got* it, *flaunt* it, I say. I just wish *I* had it, so I could *flaunt* it, too!"

Jemima giggled, and then hushed her. "*Quiet*, Ruth! Be careful what you say! Debby is hanging around somewhere, and if she hears you, you'll find yourself having to explain to your parents! I love my sister, but she's the biggest tattletale –"

A rustling in the bushes, about a stone's throw away, make Jemima break off. Sure enough, Deborah's scowling face materialized out of the leaves.

"So that's where you're hiding! Mamm says come and help her with lunch, Jemima. And you, too, Ruth -- *since you're here*!" Debby added rudely, and stalked off.

Jemima went red with embarrassment. She turned to her friend apologetically. "I'm sorry, Ruth," she stammered, "she's just so... *mean* these days. I don't know what's come over her!"

Ruth stood up, brushing grass from her skirt. "*I* do!" she replied tartly. She looked at Jemima's distressed face and bit back the rest of what she'd been planning to say. "But I'll be glad to help *you* with lunch."

Jemima clasped her friend's arm warmly. "*Of course* you'll stay and eat with us," she pressed, and Ruth's expression relaxed. She nodded.

They hugged one another, and walked back to the house arm in arm.

But while they were in the kitchen, dutifully making sandwiches, there was a jaunty knock at the front door.

Samuel Kauffman stuck his head into the living room and smiled. "Knock knock! Is anybody home?"

"Why, Samuel," Rachel King exclaimed in a pleased tone, "come in! I hope everything is well with your folks?"

"They're fine," Samuel smiled.

The girls craned their necks to sneak a look at Samuel as he began to chat with Jemima's mother. Samuel towered over her, and he had taken his hat off in deference. His blond hair shone like summer wheat.

Ruth squeezed Jemima's arm in excitement, and they both smothered giggles.

"He's here to see you – lucky thing!" Ruth hissed.

Jemima blushed and smoothed her hair back, but to her consternation, her mother was saying:

"Well, Samuel, in that case, you'll have to go out to the shop and talk to Jacob. He won't let you court with Jemima unless you talk to him first."

Ruth hissed, "Did you hear that?"

Jemima put her hands over her mouth, and her heart began to beat oddly. She stopped even pretending to make sandwiches and inclined her ear to catch every word spoken.

"Thank you, Rachel," Samuel said in a respectful tone, and took his leave.

After the door closed behind him, Jemima's mother returned to the kitchen. She was trying hard to project a calm demeanor, but Jemima could see at once that her mother was on fire with excitement.

Jemima's eyes went to her mother's face. She searched it silently.

Rachel King broke down. "He wants to *court* with you, Jemima," she said thrillingly. "The second boy in as many *days*! Your father will be –"

But another quick knock at the door interrupted her words. They all turned to look through the kitchen door.

Another young man stood hat in hand on the doorstep.

Jemima looked at her mother worriedly. Her admirers were dropping by so often now that it was becoming almost *awkward*.

Rachel King took a deep breath, smoothed her apron, and went back out to greet their newest guest.

That evening at dinner, Jacob King put a forkful of potatoes into his mouth, and gave his lovely daughter a rueful glance.

"*Four* now," he told her, and Jemima turned a guilty red.

He turned to his wife. "What am I going to do with her?" he asked, with a twinkle in his eye. "If this keeps up, we're going to have to make them take *numbers*. I thought Samuel Kauffman and that what's-his-name Beiler boy were going to fight each other on the porch today."

Rachel smiled at Jemima. "Jemima is a *very* blessed young lady," she murmured happily. "Jemima, you should be praying every day for wisdom. You have an… unusual choice ahead of you. It isn't many girls who have so many suitors to choose from."

Deborah had been listening to the conversation in unhappy silence, but apparently she had endured her limit. She twisted her freckled face into a scowl and cried: "Jemima, Jemima, *Jemima*! If I hear one more word about *Jemima* and her *boyfriends*, I'm going to *throw up*!" She jumped up, flounced out of the room, and slammed the door behind her.

Jacob watched her, and frowned, but didn't seem disposed to interrupt his meal. He took another bite of ham. "Do you want me to get involved?" he asked quietly, and looked at his wife.

Rachel closed her eyes, but shook her head. "No. I'll take

care of it. I know what it is. She's going through an awkward phase, and the boys at school tease her. It's hard for her, and then to be compared to Jemima -- But I *can't wait* until she's fourteen, and over this – this –" She gave a soft huff, rose, and followed her daughter.

That left Jemima alone with her father. She raised her eyes tentatively to his face.

His expression softened as he looked down at her. "Well, Mima, you've got all the boys in this county rushing to my door! Got any that you want me to throw *back*?"

He winked and laughed, and Jemima blushed and sputtered, "Oh, *Daed*."

After dinner, Jemima went up to her bedroom and sat at the window. She brushed her glowing hair and looked out through the green curtain of trees. The window was open and a cool breath of air, smelling of mown grass, wafted in.

She really should be putting the finishing touches on her work. She had sewn three big boxes full of dolls to sell at the store in town. There was a big summer festival planned for the next morning, and she was going to have to get up early to get them to town before the shop opened.

Jemima sighed and looked down at the neatly stitched cloth dolls. There was a blank space where their faces would have been, as was Amish tradition.

She looked out through the trees again. She felt like a doll sometimes herself, only uncomfortably different – like the one *painted* doll in a box full of normal ones.

She put the brush down and sighed.

She couldn't concentrate on even the simplest task these days.

If she stared out the window long enough, she began to see faces – Mark Christner's strong face, and Samuel Kauffman's laughing one, and even Joseph Beiler's shy eyes.

Mark was strong and sure and steady and handsome and she knew him so well and was so comfortable with him.

Samuel was fun and easy to talk to and he made her laugh and he was always interesting.

Joseph was quiet and shy, but so handsome, and, she thought -- *very* smitten.

How could she choose between them? She couldn't bear the thought of hurting Mark -- *or* Samuel. And Joseph was so sweet and quiet.

She looked up at the soft twilit sky. Lord, what should I do? she prayed. I wouldn't hurt any of them for the world, but I'll have to, if I choose one over the others. Please show me what You want me to do.

She glanced back over her shoulder. She could hear the muffled sound of Deborah making noise in her own bedroom, across the hall. It sounded like she was muttering angrily and kicking something.

And please give me patience with Debby, Lord. Sometimes I have un-Christian thoughts about her.

There was a crash, and what sounded like a curse word, from across the hall. Then Deborah shrieked out, removing any doubt. There was a thunderous stomping sound, and Jemima's door burst open to reveal her angry sister.

"*Why* didn't you tell me that this clock you gave me was a piece of junk?" she demanded, throwing it down on Jemima's bed. "It just fell apart! I'm *tired* of getting all *your* old hand-me –"

Their mother appeared suddenly in the hall, her anxious eyes on Deborah's scowling face. "Deborah, that's no way to talk to your sister. I won't have you behaving like this. Go back to your room."

Deborah pinched her lips together and stomped out again.

Jemima met her mother's eyes ruefully, and they exchanged an unspoken comment before Rachel King sighed and closed Jemima's door after her.

Jemima turned to her work and closed up the big cardboard boxes. Then she turned down the lamp and undressed for bed.

Tomorrow morning was going to start early.

CHAPTER FOUR

The next morning Jemima stood outside, shivering in the early morning chill. The lanterns on the buggy threw off a ghostly light in the predawn darkness.

Her father came striding out across the porch to the buggy, and his big shoes made a thunderous sound. When he climbed up into the driver's seat, the whole buggy leaned to one side.

He stuck his head out. "Hoist the boxes up, Mima," he told her, and held out his hands.

Jemima lifted up the boxes, and he stacked them in the back seat of the buggy. Then he extended his big hand, and Jemima took it. One pull from his muscular arm was all it took to catapult her into the seat. She shrieked, and laughed, and almost went tumbling into her father's arms.

"Steady on," he told her indulgently. "All in?"

She adjusted her cap and nodded, and he flicked the whip.

Their dark chestnut, Rufus, swished his tail and started down the road at a smart clip.

"I have some business to do in town," Jacob told her, "But I'll only be gone for a few minutes. I'll park outside the store, and meet you there when I'm done. I should be there before you're finished."

Jemima nodded.

"Have you decided what you're going to do with the money, Mima?" he teased her.

Jemima shook her head. "Save it, I suppose," she told him.

"That's a smart girl," he replied approvingly. "You'll likely *need* the extra money before the year is out."

Jemima smiled, and went pink.

By the time they had reached town, the sun was just rising. At that early hour, the shopkeepers and festival organizers were the only ones in town. A few people were raising a big tent in the town square, and vendors were setting up tables in preparation for the crowd.

There was even a truck with a news logo on the door parked on the far side of the block, and seeing it, Jacob muttered impatiently and turned Rufus' head. The buggy disappeared down a side street.

"You can knock on the back door of the shop," Jacob told her. "I'll stay until Mr. Satterwhite lets you in."

Jemima jumped down from the buggy and knocked softly on the back door. After a few minutes Mr. Satterwhite opened it and greeted her with: "Up early, eh, Jemima? Got some dolls for me?"

Jemima smiled and nodded.

"Well, I'll help you get them in. I expect they'll sell out quick, with all the folks expected in town today."

When they had carried all the dolls inside, her father raised his hand. "I'll be back in a few minutes, Jemima," he called.

Jemima put up her hand and then returned to the shop.

Mr. Satterwhite closed the back door behind her, and led her through the stock room up to the sales floor. He put the cardboard boxes on the counter. "So, three boxes, that makes 30 dolls this time, I guess," he muttered. "That's $150 American." He opened the cash register and counted out some bills.

Jemima drifted away from the counter as he talked. She let her eyes wander idly over the merchandise – mostly rustic knick-knacks, handmade quilts and crafts, like her dolls, and a smattering of antiques. She picked up a little stuffed rabbit with floppy ears and smiled into its button eyes.

"Here you go, Jemima," Mr. Satterwhite called.

She put down the stuffed toy and went to the counter. The elderly man counted the money out and put it into an envelope. "You do good work, Jemima," he told her. "If this batch sells as well as the others, I'll want three boxes every month."

Jemima smiled at him. "Thank you, Mr. Satterwhite." She tucked the envelope into a little bag. "Would you like me to open the front door for you?"

He craned his neck, looking out through the shop windows. "Thank you, yes, it is getting on toward opening. Go ahead."

Jemima walked to the shop doors and threw them open. The square was beginning to come alive with food and art vendors. Someone was setting up a P.A. system, and was testing the mic. The first festivalgoers were beginning to arrive.

She turned back, and her eye was caught by a small wooden wall clock sitting in a cardboard box by the door. It was plain and looked old, but it was made of a rich cherry wood, and the dial looked hand painted. Its fine, curving numerals scrolled delicately over the yellowed dial.

She picked it up, turned it over in her hands, and remembered Deborah's tantrum about her broken clock. She smiled ruefully. It probably *was* hard on her, to have to live with so many hand-me-downs.

She looked up at Mr. Satterwhite. "Is this clock for sale?" she asked.

He squinted. "That old thing? My wife got it at an auction

yesterday. I haven't really decided what to charge for it. I can't imagine it would bring much. Why, were you interested in it?"

Jemima looked down at it. "I was thinking I might buy it for my sister."

"Well... I guess you could have it for five dollars, if you want it."

Jemima brought it up to the counter, and handed the shop owner a five dollar bill. He scribbled out a receipt, and she stuck it into her bag.

"To tell you the truth, I don't know why you want it," he said candidly.

"Oh, I don't know," Jemima answered softly. "I think it's pretty. It has a – a *look*. As if it's been worn *soft*."

"Hmm." He looked over her head and nodded. "Looks like your father is back."

Jemima turned to see the buggy parked on the street outside. She picked up the clock and nestled it in the crook of her arm. "Thank you, Mr. Satterwhite. I'll have your order for you next month at the same time."

He threw up his hand and she walked out of the store.

The square outside was coming alive with people. A band had started to pick out notes over the P.A. system, and the scent of funnel cakes sweetened the air. Jemima turned her eyes in the direction of the music, and took them off of where she was going.

A sharp, sudden collision brought her back to her surroundings – too late. She smacked into another pedestrian, *hard*. The clock jumped out of her arms, fell on the sidewalk, and cracked open.

Jemima put her hand to her mouth in dismay. "Oh *no!*" she wailed.

She lifted her eyes to the other person, and found two bright, humorous eyes trained on hers.

"I'm so sorry!" the man said apologetically. He bent down to pick up the clock. "I didn't see you coming. Here's your clock." He picked up the pieces and handed them to her. "It looks like the back popped off, but I don't think it's broken." His eyes returned to the sidewalk. "I think this came out, too." He bent down and picked up a folded piece of paper.

Jemima took it from his outstretched hand, and looked up fleetingly into his face. The stranger had light blue eyes shining from underneath bushy brown eyebrows, a wry, strong mouth, and a thick mop of curly, brown-blonde hair.

Her glance flitted down. To her horror, he was wearing a blue oxford with the logo of a local *newspaper* stitched into the collar.

She turned without a word and jumped up into the buggy, and her father whipped up the horse instantly. Rufus jumped into a canter, and the buggy lurched away. Jemima hugged the clock to her chest. Her heart was pounding.

But when she looked back over her shoulder at the shop entrance, the stranger was still standing on the sidewalk, staring after her.

CHAPTER FIVE

Brad Williams stood in the middle of the street, staring open mouthed at the retreating buggy. The delicate, luminous redhead riding away inside of it was quite possibly the most beautiful woman he'd ever seen in his life. His lips pursed in a soundless whistle.

They do grow everything better here, he thought wryly, and shook his head. Must be something in the water.

An irritable voice intruded on his amazement. "Don't block the entryway." An elderly shopkeeper was staring at him, hands on hips.

"Oh – oh, yeah. I was just coming in for a bite of breakfast. You do sell food, right?"

Mr. Satterwhite jerked a thumb in the direction of the counter. "In the mini-fridge to the right. I have soda and some cheese danish."

"Coffee?"

"On the counter."

The young man sauntered to the front of the shop and poured black coffee into a paper cup. He took an appreciative sip and looked around the store. "I'm Brad Williams from the *Ledger*. Do you mind if I ask you a few questions about the festival?" he asked.

Mr. Satterwhite picked up a broom and started sweeping the floor. "Yes, I mind."

Brad looked at him and cracked a grin. "Have a little pity, friend. It's a slow day."

"And it will be until you leave," the elderly man replied bluntly. "Folks around here don't like reporters."

"Oh, I don't bite. Think about it, anyway. *Free publicity*."

"I don't need publicity, young man. My customers already know where I am."

Brad grinned again, took a danish out of the mini-fridge, and slapped a ten dollar bill into the man's outstretched hand.

"Now get along, you'll hex me," Mr. Satterwhite told him, counting out change.

Brad took a bite of the cheese danish and sauntered out into the doorway. He stood there momentarily, chewing, and so was almost knocked down for the second time that morning.

A big man in a business suit came charging into the shop, knocking him to one side. He stopped in front of the store counter and stood there, flushed and breathless. When he caught sight of Mr. Satterwhite, he demanded: "Are you the owner here?"

The elderly man gave him a withering glance. "Yes, I am," he replied.

Brad called indignantly from the doorway: "Hey, buster, why don't you *knock me down* next time?" he objected, brushing frosting off his shirt. "I should send you the cleaning bill for this!"

The man ignored him. He sighed deeply, caught his breath, and trained his dark eyes on Mr. Satterwhite. "Did you buy a clock yesterday, at an estate auction in Marietta?"

The elderly man looked at him narrowly. "My wife bought a bunch of junk at an auction yesterday," he drawled. "I think there was a clock."

The man stared at him intently. *"Do you still have it?"*

Mr. Satterwhite shook his head. "Nope. I sold it this morning."

The man stifled an impatient exclamation and asked, *"Who did you sell it to?"*

Brad, who was still brushing his shirt front in the doorway, looked up at this.

The elderly man bristled. "That's none of your business, mister," he replied, with a straight look.

The man shook his head. "I'm sorry. It's just that the auction was for my mother's estate, and the clock was important to me for sentimental reasons. I would be willing to pay whatever the person gave for it, and a little more. Do you know the person who bought it? Would you be willing to give them that message for me, or, tell me how to contact them, so I can ask myself?"

"I know the girl who bought it, but I'm not going to give out her name without her permission," Mr. Satterwhite replied coldly.

"So she lives around here?"

"Look here, I've answered all the questions I'm going to this morning," Mr. Satterwhite snapped. "Buy something, or get out! I have work to do."

The man held up his hands. "All right, all right. But I'm going to write down my name and number. Can you at least give her this, and ask her to call me, when you see her again? I'd appreciate it."

Brad narrowed his eyes and walked back into the store. He leaned against one wall with his arms crossed.

The older man appeared somewhat mollified. "I'll take it,

but I'm not promising you anything."

"Thank you. I appreciate it." The man put his pen back into his jacket pocket and glanced at Brad as he walked out.

"Sorry about the shirt," he apologized, and hurried off.

Brad watched him as he walked down the street.

"He sure was anxious to get his hands on that clock," he murmured, mostly to himself. He turned to Mr. Satterwhite. "That girl I bumped into when I first came in – the redhead – was that her?"

The older man shrugged, and refused to answer. Brad smiled and shook a forefinger.

"It *was* her! What's her name?"

The old man lifted angry eyes. "I'm not telling *you*, any more than I told him! Now beat it!"

"Okay, but at least tell me where she lives. Hey, you wouldn't give me an interview, at least help me get one for myself!"

Mr. Satterwhite set his mouth. "Okay -- if it will get you out of here! She lives ten miles away from town. You take Yoder Road out to the river, and –"

"Wait, wait," Brad interrupted, scrambling for a pen. "Okay, what again?"

"You cross the river, and take the first right on the river

road. You have to look close – it's an unmarked, dirt road. You follow it for five miles, and then take the second left – you'll know it by the big oak tree – and her father's farm is the third one on that road. A big house with green shutters."

"Got it." Brad snapped the pen and grinned. "Thanks!"

The old man nodded grimly, and watched his customer stride out and disappear into the crowd.

Then he laughed to himself, a dry, cackling laugh, and wiped his eyes.

CHAPTER SIX

Brad Williams moved through the crowd toward the company truck. His cameraman was still sitting in it. The other man looked up as Brad approached, and relief flooded his face.

"There you are! Where you been, man? I've been sitting here for thirty minutes! Do you have something lined up?"

Brad opened the car door and slid in. "I have a new lead. Here's the game plan. Get plenty of crowd shots, lots of generic local color, and I'll fill in the blanks when I get back."

"You're taking the truck? We're supposed to be working the festival!"

"I've got a lead on something more interesting."

The cameraman shook his head. "Man, Delores is going to have your hide."

Brad winked and grinned. "Delores loves me."

"Yeah, you're going to find out how much she loves you," the other man retorted, wrestling with his camera equipment. "I am so glad, that I am not *you*."

"I'll be back, Eddie!" Brad called after him.

"Wait, how long are you going to be gone?"

But the roar of the truck engine was the only answer he got. The cameraman slumped, and shook his head, and hoisted his equipment on his shoulder. He was still muttering to himself as he disappeared into the crowd.

It took fifteen minutes of crawling traffic to get out of the festival traffic, but once he was clear, Brad stuck the piece of paper on the truck dashboard and squinted at the handwriting.

"Yoder Road…where the heck…okay, okay, there it is." He made a left turn onto a long, straight two-lane road that plunged immediately into corn fields, and stayed there for fifteen minutes. The only signs of life on it were the occasional Amish buggy, and guys out working the fields.

He squinted at the paper again. "Stay on Yoder Road until the river…what river? Where is the stupid – okay, coming up."

There was a wide, shallow river visible on the road ahead. There was a bridge, and barely visible beyond it, a tiny, unmarked dirt road. Brad thought dryly that it was just as well that the old man had warned him, because he never would have noticed it otherwise. He made a hard right turn and the truck plunged onto the dirt road, kicking up a trail of dust.

"Okay…follow it for five miles, and take the second left…big oak tree."

The truck bounced along the dirt road, jouncing over potholes and the occasional rock. The only things visible on it were a line of trees overhanging the river, on the right, and dense forest on the left. There wasn't even a house now.

At the five mile mark, just as the directions said, there was a huge old oak tree on the left side of the road, and a turning onto another, even smaller, dirt road. He turned left, and consulted the paper again.

"Third farm on the road…big house…green shutters."

He drove down the road, which was getting progressively worse. The potholes were getting bigger and harder to navigate. He craned his neck, looking for a farm, but there were only more and bigger trees, crowding more and more closely to the edge of the road.

At last he pulled the truck to a stop. The sign across the road read, *Dead End.*

He groaned and pressed his head against the wheel.

An hour later Brad Williams walked into the Satterwhite

Gift Shop, tired, rumpled, and grim.

"*Ha ha*," he said sardonically.

Mr. Satterwhite smirked, and continued scribbling in a ledger. "I told you I wasn't going to give you information, boy," he said dryly. "You should learn to take a hint."

Brad slumped against the wall, and eyed him. "Look, what if that clock turns out to be something valuable, and your friend doesn't know it? That guy sure sounded anxious to get it back."

"What's your interest in it?" the old man drawled.

"A story, of course."

The old man shook his head. "You're new here, aren't you boy? None of the Amish folk are going to talk to you."

Brad sighed, bit his lip, and turned to go, but couldn't resist a parting shot.

"*You* can still do an interview though, right?"

"Get out!"

Brad walked out onto the street and into a running stream of tourists. He shielded his eyes, squinting. There might still be time to get a few good interviews before the festival was over for the day, and he had to go back to the paper. To report to his editor, *Delores*.

He bit his lip.

With yet another boring story about a vegetable festival in Amish country.

It was true that he was fresh out of school, a greenhorn reporter, but Delores hadn't assigned him anything more important than horse auctions and business openings since he arrived.

It was *past* time for something more substantial.

He rolled a pen between his fingers. The clock thing was intriguing, and possibly newsworthy, if his hunch was right. And if the clock turned out to be something old or valuable, a story about it might help him move up from the grunt assignments, to actual *news*.

His mind returned to the redheaded beauty. The old man at the store had been tough as an old boot, but maybe one of the other shop owners in town would know who the girl was, and be willing to give a name, at least.

And he had to admit, the prospect of seeing her again was hardly less pleasant than that of getting a good story.

He wiped his brow with one arm, straightened, and walked into the store to the left of the Satterwhite Gift Shop.

"Yes, she comes into town every so often to sell her dolls."

The woman behind the counter was plump, matronly, and, to Brad's relief, fond of talking.

"Do you know her name?"

"Oh yes, her name is Jemima King. Pretty little thing, all the Amish boys are wild about her."

Brad nodded pleasantly. "I guess she must be a local, then."

"Yes, her family has lived here for hundreds of years! Her father has a blacksmith shop about five miles out of town."

"Could you tell me how to get there?"

She giggled. "If you're hoping to get a date, young man, you'll be disappointed. Her father will never let her go out with a young man who isn't Amish!"

"Oh, it's not that," he smiled. "I just wanted to ask a question."

She shook her head and smiled. "You can try, but you'll most likely be wasting a trip." She looked at him amiably, and began scribbling out directions on a piece of paper.

CHAPTER SEVEN

The next morning, Brad tapped on the steering wheel of the truck and whistled as it zoomed over the back roads. The news truck was drawing startled looks from the Amish passersby, but there were few on the roads at that hour. Most were in fields or workshops at that time of day.

Brad consulted the directions the shop lady had given him, and to his relief, this time they were correct. As she had described, there was the King farm: an immaculate white farm house, surrounded by a green patchwork of garden plots and fields.

Brad pulled the truck into the long driveway to the farm, but to his surprise, there was already a car in the drive.

Even *he* knew that a car at an Amish house meant that *something was up*.

He pulled in behind the car and got out. There was movement on the farmhouse porch. The redheaded girl was standing there, looking even better than he remembered. But to his astonishment – and suspicion – the businessman he had seen at the store was there, too. He was gesturing earnestly toward the girl. Brad scrambled out of the car and strode up to the house.

"Hi there!" he called to her, putting up a hand. "Remember me? We met at the store yesterday, by accident. My name is Brad Williams."

He bounded up the porch steps and smiled big and bright. The girl's luminous green eyes met his doubtfully, and made his skin tingle in the places they swept.

The other man turned to him impatiently. "Look, kid, why don't you get out of here," he snapped. "This is none of *your* business, after all. This young lady was about to sell me my mother's clock." He stuck a handful of cash towards her.

For the first time, Brad noticed that the girl was holding the old clock that had fallen on the sidewalk. He frowned and looked up at her.

"Look, miss, I don't know you, but I came out here to ask you about this clock. Don't sell it just yet. Do you remember that when you dropped it, and the back popped open, that a paper fell out? I just wanted to ask you what it was. Have you looked at the paper?"

The girl frowned, and shook her head.

"Well," he added gently, "don't you think you *should* look

at the paper, before you sell the clock? You never know. Sometimes little things like that turn out to be important." He shot a dry look at the other man. "Or *valuable!*"

"That clock is worthless to anybody but me," the businessman interjected. "I'm doing you a favor, young lady, by offering you a profit. I hope you don't plan to take advantage of the situation!"

Brad shot him an unfriendly glance. "You're awfully eager," he observed. "I wonder why?"

"Miss, we have an agreement," the other man said, in an irritated tone. "I expect you to honor your promise!"

She looked at him, and spoke for the first time. Brad was alarmed to discover that the sound of her voice was like velvet against his ear, and made it difficult to concentrate on what she was actually saying. He shook his head slightly, as if to recalibrate it.

"No, I didn't promise," she replied doubtfully. "You said you wanted to *see* the clock, and I told you I'd bring it out."

Her eyes moved back to Brad. "What do you want to ask me about it?"

His eyes lingered wistfully on hers. He smiled again, a bit crookedly. "I just want to know what the paper is."

"Why?"

"I work for a newspaper. There might be a story in it."

Instantly, he was conscious of having made a mistake. She pulled the clock to her chest, and for an instant he was afraid that she would run inside the house. She shook her head.

"No, I won't be in the paper. I won't have my picture taken!" she replied firmly.

Brad put up his hands. "Okay, I get it, I respect that," he answered quickly. "But can you at least just satisfy my curiosity? I'd really like to know what the paper is."

"You have no business being here at all!" the other man broke out savagely.

Brad met his glare steadily. "As much as you, friend," he replied through his teeth.

The girl looked first at the businessman and then back at him. Finally she looked down at the clock, and opened the back panel. A small, yellowed piece of paper fell out into her hands.

She unfolded it.

"It's a letter," she said simply and then frowned.

"From who?" Brad moved as close as he dared.

She was staring at the paper as if she couldn't believe her eyes. "*George Washington*," she replied, in a stunned tone.

In spite of himself, Brad leaned over and snatched it out of her hands. He looked down at it in amazement. Sure enough, there was the signature. He raised his eyes to hers, and smiled apologetically as he handed it back.

"I'm sorry, miss, that was rude of me. It's just that – do you know how *valuable* this might be?"

"This is outrageous!" the other man exploded. "That clock belonged to my mother for years, and by rights, it belongs to me now! Take the money, and give me my clock!" He threw a handful of bills down at her feet.

With one swift step, Brad moved between the other man and the girl. "Hey, leave her alone!"

The other man suddenly stepped up and drew his fist back. The girl screamed, and Brad put up his arms to block the blow.

But he was spared the necessity.

A huge redheaded man suddenly loomed up behind the businessman, grabbed him by the shoulders, and flung him a good fifteen feet out onto the lawn. The man hit the ground rolling, scrambled up, fell, got up again, and ran for his life.

He jumped into his car. It roared to life and scratched off down the road in a frenzied cloud of dust.

Then the flame-haired giant turned around. He was wearing a grim expression that Brad had no trouble interpreting.

He eyes widened. He put up his hands. "Okay, I'm leaving.

I am going *now*." He backed warily around the other man, and down the porch.

But as he left, he called out, "Miss, I'm telling you, you should have that letter appraised. If it's real, it could be worth a *fortune*! You might be rich –"

The older man made as if to come after him, and he turned and beat a hasty retreat.

But he turned at the car door and called out again. "*Have it appraised*!"

Then the big man came striding across the lawn after him, and he was obliged to beat the second hasty retreat of the morning.

CHAPTER EIGHT

Brad put a hand to his chest, and it reflexively fumbled for his shirt pocket before he remembered that he was trying to give up cigarettes, and that there were none there. He muttered under his breath.

His heart was still pounding from the adrenaline rush of a fight-or-flight morning, but it was also jumping with excitement. His instinct had been right: there *had* been a big story in that strange little clock.

He chewed his lip. Now if he could only get that girl alone, and convince her to have the letter appraised, it might be a story that could go viral. He could already see the headline: *Amish beauty strikes it rich.* Or maybe, *Local antique hides priceless find.*

Because that was probably the truth. Why else would that other guy have gone to so much trouble to track down an old, ugly clock? And why would anyone hide the letter in the first place, unless they *believed* at least that it was genuine?

He was already rehearsing his speech to Delores.

Delores, you won't believe what I just found.

No, that sounded eager.

Delores, I could be sitting on the biggest story this paper has seen for years.

His mouth twisted. She'd probably crack an obscene joke.

Delores, I have an intriguing lead. I want your okay to check it out.

Yes, that was better. She might go for that.

He reached for a cigarette again, didn't find one again, and mumbled in disgust.

"You *what?*"

Delores Watkins put her hand on one ample hip and tilted her head to one side in incredulous wonder.

"It could be *legit,* Delores. Think of it – a letter from George Washington, a national *treasure,* possibly worth hundreds of thousands of dollars, found in a local shop!"

"Are you crazy?"

"I saw it. It was on some kind of parchment-type paper, it was yellow, and the ink had gone brown. It looked *genuine.*"

She closed her eyes, pursed her lips, and nodded her head. "Sure, sure. *Genuine*. Like the time you wanted to go with the story that the mayor might be descended from Teddy Roosevelt."

Brad looked away in irritation. "Can I help it if the guy falsified documents? And I wasn't the only one who believed him – it actually *ran* on Channel 3!"

Delores shook her head. "Let it be a lesson to you, to check it five times before you come to me." She turned and walked away.

Brad moved to keep pace. "And that's what I *want* to do with this story. I want the green light to follow up, to have it checked out. Let me go back there. If I can convince the girl to have the letter appraised, and it turns out to be genuine, we'll have something that could go *viral* online. If it's not genuine, who cares? It'll just be a few hours lost."

"*And* money. I'm assuming you want the paper to pay for this?"

"Hey, does the paper want me to work for free? I'm telling you, Delores, this could be huge. *I held the letter in my hand. The signature at the bottom read George Washington.*"

"And the tab on the back of my shirt reads *Valentino Tucci*. I bought it at a dollar store."

"Delores, just let me try. *Three days*. If she says no, I come back, and no harm done. If she says *yes* –"

His boss fixed him with ironic brown eyes. "--then we'll all be amazed," she finished sardonically. "Go back to your desk already, Brad. You're nuts."

Delores walked off, leaving him to stare after her. He bowed his head in frustration, and rubbed the back of his neck.

Then he looked up, and noticed that everybody else in the office was looking at him.

"Ah, shut up!" he mumbled good-naturedly, and giggling filled the room.

The next day, Delores Watkins looked up from her desk to see Brad Williams hovering over it.

"Delores, what if I foot the bill myself?" he asked, eyes on her face.

She looked up with a dry expression in her eyes. "I know what you make. You don't have *that* much money."

"I mean it. If I bomb, I eat the expense – the hotel, the appraisal, everything. If I score – *metaphorically* speaking," he grinned "then the paper reimburses me for my expenses."

"That girl must be pin-up material," Delores observed, in an amused tone.

Brad flushed red, but rallied: "She's a gorgeous green-eyed

redhead. She's photogenic as *he–* she's photogenic," he said quickly.

He leaned in close and hissed, "Picture the page views for *Amish Barbie Gets Rich*! I'm telling you, it will play like a Stradivarius, and all I have to do is get the confirmation that the letter is genuine. What do you have to lose?"

Dolores twirled a pencil between bright orange nails. "Okay, Romeo. Three days. Not that I believe it for a minute, but if you're willing to foot the bill – okay. *Go.* Knock yourself out."

Brad cracked a wide grin. "You love me, Delores -- admit it!" He leaned over and kissed her cheek.

She turned it toward him, but retorted, "I tolerate you. And guess what? I still expect you to finish your other assignments, while you're gone."

"I'm on it," he called, but was already backing out of the office. He pointed a jubilant finger at the older woman. "*You won't be sorry, Delores!*"

"I'm sorry already."

Brad hurried off to his desk and rummaged around in the upper drawer. He grabbed a thumb drive, and a camera.

Another reporter watched him with a jaundiced eye. "So Delores finally gave in, eh?"

"She knows I'm right," Brad told him.

"Fifty dollars says you'll strike out. No Amish woman is going to agree to meet a strange English man -- let alone a reporter!"

"You're on. And you're going to lose your money. You know why, my friend?"

The other man rested his chin on his hands. "Enlighten me."

"Because I'm going to help that girl get *rich*," he replied. He looked up and grinned. "*And* because women *love* me."

The other man threw an eraser at his head. "Get out of here!"

CHAPTER NINE

Brad closed the truck door, brushed the crumbs of his dinner off of his shirt, and surveyed the underwhelming exterior of Uncle Bob's Amish Motel. It was a long, low, red brick structure that looked as if was a remodeled '60s restaurant.

He sighed, locked the truck door, and went in.

The teenaged girl behind the counter was chewing gum and listening to an mp3. She brightened when he walked in, and pulled the earphones out.

"Hi, can I help you?" she smiled.

Brad dug out his wallet. "Yeah, I'd like a single room for three nights." He opened up the slender billfold and looked down at it despondently. "The chea— the most *economical* room available."

The girl dimpled at him, and consulted her computer screen. "I have a single room available for $50 a night, but it's next to the laundry room, and it may be noisy sometimes. Is that okay?"

"That's perfect. You have wi-fi, right?"

"Oh, yes."

He pushed a card across the counter, and her hand brushed his as she took it. She giggled and tossed her head slightly.

Brad glanced around. The lobby was spare, but looked clean, and the room beyond was, apparently, a *very* basic dining room. He tilted his head to the right. "Is breakfast included in the price of a room?"

"You get a Continental breakfast: coffee, juice, fruit and danish," she recited.

"That's great."

She handed him a receipt and a room key. "Your room is on the right, past the dining room. First turn to the left, and the fifth door on the left."

"Thanks."

"If you need anything, just call me," she sang out.

He smiled faintly, and waved.

When he opened the door to Room 205, he was greeted by the loud hum of an air conditioner, a blast of cold, and an aggressive floral scent that was certainly cheap air freshener. There was a single bed, neatly made, a desk with a chair, and a bathroom.

He walked to the desk and set up his laptop then pulled the curtains open with a *snap*. He was startled to see a black cow looking back at him. It stood there, eyeing him patiently, over the fence that separated the motel from the neighboring farm.

He unlocked the window and threw it open, and nodded to the cow. "Howdy there, bossy," he told it. "Got time for a few questions?"

The cow turned her head and looked off into the distance.

He nodded. "What is it with people around here, *hmm*? If I didn't know better, I'd say you were being unfriendly."

He plopped down on the bed, put his hands behind his head, and stared up at the ceiling.

Now that he had Delores's okay, the next step in his plan was to find a way to persuade that curvy redheaded girl to get the letter appraised.

He'd been so preoccupied with winning Delores over that he hadn't had time to think of much else, but he had to admit, the prospect of seeing that girl again was a distinctly pleasant one -- quite apart from the story.

Of course, getting her alone wasn't going to be easy.

He called her up again in his mind. Her eyes were the lightest, most startling green he'd ever seen. They were as big and beautiful as a cat's, ringed with thick black lashes, and slightly almond-shaped.

They stood out like – he couldn't think of the right words -- like *green jewels on white satin.*

He caught himself, and his mouth curled down. He was waxing *poetic.*

But still.

And the look in them had been so... soft. *Gentle*, that was the word.

He fumbled in his shirt pocket, and this time, there was a pack of cigarettes in it. He lighted one, and puffed contemplatively.

Yes, she was a beauty, all right.

Her dress seemed designed to cover up her figure – that Amish prudishness – but even so, it couldn't completely hide the fact that she was young, lissome, and graceful.

He blew a spout of smoke toward the ceiling.

But also, *extremely* shy. And guarded by an angry giant who he assumed to be her father.

The memory of the man's expression gave him real pause. It didn't take a rocket scientist to know that if that guy caught him out there talking to his daughter, he was going to need his insurance plan.

But still, her father couldn't stay with her *all* the time. There had to be some window of opportunity, and he was determined to find it.

He frowned.

It was a beautiful place, that farm. Just setting aside what had happened there, or even that an uber-hot girl lived in it. It looked peaceful. Well-ordered.

And it was clear that the girl had a parent who was there all the time, and willing to protect her.

His face twisted. *Sweet setup.* Something like that would've been nice when *he* was a kid.

He crushed the cigarette butt into an ashtray.

If he could just find some way to get to that girl, to get her alone, he had a shot. She looked as if she'd be fairly pliable. If he could convince her that the letter might bring a lot of money, *and* that he'd pay the fee for the appraisal, she might agree.

The appraisal. He pulled his hands over his face. It was going to cost hundreds of dollars, money he didn't have.

But it was a risk he was willing to take.

Because if the letter proved to be real, it would make his

name famous overnight and then maybe he could start getting the *real* assignments, and leave the boonies behind forever.

Wouldn't do that girl any harm, either.

Maybe then she'd be able to afford to see the real world, and get a life of her own.

CHAPTER TEN

Jemima clutched the clock to her chest, watching in consternation as the newspaper reporter twisted round in front of his truck and yelled to her:

"If it's real, it could be worth a *fortune*! You might be *rich*!"

She stared at him in amazement. To look at the stranger's expression, you would think that a tiny scrap of paper had created some terrible emergency – like the *world* was going to end somehow. Then her father had started toward him, and the young man had dived into the truck, cranked the motor, and drove off.

She watched the truck as it disappeared down the road, trailing dust.

Her father climbed the porch steps and paused in front of her. He put his big hands lightly on her shoulders.

"Are you all right, Mima?"

She looked up at him, and nodded mutely.

His whole body seemed to relax. He exhaled, and released her -- but planted his hands on his hips.

"Well, then, tell me -- *what* was *that*?"

She blushed, and shook her head. "I don't know, Daed. An English man wearing a fancy suit came out this morning asking to buy this clock –" she presented it to him – "the clock I bought in town, because he said it belonged to his mother. I went to get it, but before I could sell it to him, a newspaper reporter drove up and told me not to sell the clock, because it might be valuable."

Jacob King tilted his head to one side and studied at the clock doubtfully. "It looks plain enough to me," he observed, picking it up and turning it back and forth.

"Oh, but it's not the clock itself, Daed," Jemima said earnestly, "it's the letter that was hidden inside. *Look*." She handed the little yellowed note to her father.

He read it, and his frown deepened. He uttered a deep, skeptical grunt.

"Probably a prank of some kind. Pay it no mind, Mima." He handed the letter back to her. "The English are crazy, and greedy for money *always*."

He lifted his head, and gazed out over the fields in the

direction that the strangers had fled. His expression darkened.

"But if any other Englishers come back, I want you to come and get me. *I'll take care of them.*"

"Yes, Daed," Jemima murmured submissively.

"Now come and make me a sandwich, daughter," he told her, putting an arm around her shoulder. "Since my work has been interrupted, I may as well have my lunch now."

Jemima walked into the house arm in arm with her father. She set the clock down on the kitchen table, and the letter beside it then went to the refrigerator to make her father lunch.

Deborah walked in while she was doing it. Her quick eye fell at once on the clock.

"What's *that* ugly thing?"

Jacob turned to look at his youngest daughter with a warning glint in his eye. "That is the clock your sister bought for you with her own money, so you could have one to replace the one that broke," he told her sternly.

Deborah picked it up and flipped it contemptuously. "It'll probably be broken, too, in a few weeks," she complained. "It looks a hundred years old! I *never* get any new things!"

"Enough!" Jacob thundered, and stood up.

Jemima looked up at her father in dismay, and even

Deborah knew better than to open her mouth when her father's good humor finally ran out.

"That's the last word of complaint from your mouth, Deborah," he boomed, "or next time, it won't be Scripture verses, but the *woodshed*! Don't think you're too old to be taken over my knee!"

Deborah shut her mouth with a snap.

"That's right!" her father told her sternly, and sat down, still glowering. "And because you spoke to your sister with disrespect, you can do her chores for the rest of the day."

Deborah's eyes looked as if they were ready to pop out of her head, but she remained silent. Jemima stared at her father in awed silence, and handed her sister the apron.

Rachel King came hurrying into the kitchen, drawn by the sound of her husband's voice. Her eyes went to his face, and she looked a question.

"I know what you're going to say, Rachel, and it won't work this time," he told her. "I've put up with the last bit of naughtiness from your daughter that I'm going to stand!"

"*My* daughter, Jacob?"

He looked at her, and the mild expression on her face seemed to weaken his resolve. "*Our* daughter."

She leaned over and kissed him, and he looked away, grumbling into his beard.

Rachel turned to Deborah.

"Deborah, you can make dinner tonight, too, as a reminder to watch your tongue," she said calmly.

Deborah swelled visibly, but one look at her father's simmering expression stifled the outburst.

Rachel's eyes moved to Jemima. "Jemima, you may do as you please until dinner is ready."

Jemima nodded, glanced almost fearfully at her younger sister, and moved to retrieve the clock, and the letter. She took them upstairs to her own room, and closed the door behind her.

She put the clock down on the little table beside her bed. Then she padded to the window and sank down on the floor in front of it.

She rested her head on the sill and unfolded the little letter. She hadn't had time to even read it. She had to admit that she *was* curious.

Flowing, graceful script covered the little page.

My Dearest Martha, it began, *Tonight I am thinking of our last words together before I left to begin this Great Adventure of which we are all a part. No words can express how keenly I felt the Ties between us, or how strong and entwining they are.*

Jemima put the note to her lips, smiling in surprise and delight. She had never expected a *love letter*.

A night does not pass that I do not see your Dear face when I close my eyes, or dream of you beside me. Though time and distance may part us, I feel your presence near me always, and the knowledge that your Thoughts are with me is my comfort in our present distress.

Jemima's mouth opened slightly. When and where he had written these tender words -- in a tent somewhere maybe – just before battle?

I leave to our God the outcome of our Great Struggle, and commend my soul to its Maker; but whether I go to Him tomorrow, or return to your dear side, know that your Name will be my last breath, and your face the last in my memory, when I close my eyes.

Yours ever,

G. Washington.

Jemima lowered the little note. Her mouth trembled, and her eyes filled with tears.

It was beautiful.

Her eyes returned to the page. It was the soul of a man deep in love – a man who was unsure if he would live to see his sweetheart again.

She pressed it to her chest, closed her eyes and smiled. She imagined this man coming back to his home again, and his wife running to meeting him, laughing, arms outstretched.

Then she opened her eyes again, and looked back down at it.

Her father thought the letter was an English prank, a joke. But why would anyone make up such a letter, only to hide it away?

It was so tender, so loving. Did words like *these* come from a deceitful heart?

She ran her hand lightly over the paper. Wouldn't it be *wonderful*, if it was truly a love letter from George Washington, to his Martha?

She remembered her father's words -- but he hadn't commanded her to *destroy* the letter.

She got up from the window, and walked over to the opposite wall. She ran her fingernail over the wall panel, and pushed down on one point. A tiny bit of bead board popped out to reveal a hollow space.

Jemima placed the love letter into the secret space and smiled. She thought to herself that it might not really be genuine – but that she was going to keep it, *just in case*. She carefully replaced the cover.

She told herself that she might as well keep it secret. A

calf-eyed love letter -- from *George Washington*? No one would ever believe her, if she told them!

Then she lay down on her bed, bit her fingertip and giggled.

CHAPTER ELEVEN

Jemima spent the next morning doing chores in the garden. Her mother had a vegetable patch that was an acre across, filled with the tomatoes and green peppers and onions and squash that their father loved, plus cucumbers for pickling, and pole beans.

She had a big basket, and was moving from row to row, harvesting vegetables for their meal.

A cool dawn had ripened into a perfect morning, not too hot, and slightly breezy. The air felt refreshingly cool for July, and the sky was filled with the billowy clouds of summer. Jemima shaded her eyes, thinking that they looked ripe, too – they were full and tall and blue-tinged, towering all the way to the edge of sight.

A voice from the house interrupted her reverie.

"Jemima!"

She put her basket down and smoothed her hair and skirt. It was Mark's voice.

"Here."

She could just see the top of his dark head on the other side of the garden. He waved, and came weaving through the rows of plants to reach her.

"How are you this morning?" he asked, smiling. "I haven't seen you in the last few days."

She looked down, and smiled. It felt *nice* to be missed.

"I was in town for the festival."

"You are coming to the sing this Sunday evening?"

She nodded, not looking up.

"Good. I was hoping we could talk."

She felt her cheeks going warm, but nodded again, and looked up. The shifting sunlight was moving over Mark's inky black hair, making it glisten blue.

His bright eyes were on her face. He stared at her for a long instant and then, to her surprise, he leaned over and kissed her. His lips were smooth and pleasantly warm, like the sun beaming through the dappled leaves. They moved over hers strongly, and with a steady pulse – like the thrumming of her own heart.

He took her chin in his hand. "I want to ask your Daed to

court with you," he whispered. "Would you let me, Jemima?"

She looked up into his eyes. "I – I would, Mark. *But –*"

The sound of another voice calling made Mark straighten up suddenly.

"Mark Christner!"

It was her father's voice, calling urgently – and, it seemed to his daughter, a little suspiciously.

"Yes sir!"

Mark turned to her, and took her hand in his. "Remember, Jemima. This Sunday."

"I won't forget, Mark."

"Mark!"

"I have to go." He gave her a quick peck on the cheek then turned quickly and walked back to the house.

Jemima watched him go with a little smile playing on her lips. Mark was so sweet.

She put her fingers to her lips. She liked the way he *kissed,* too.

She shook her head, and smiled. She had meant to tell Mark that Samuel had asked to court with her, as well – but she hadn't had much of a chance.

She expected that Samuel would soon be coming by to ask

her for *himself.*

She smiled again, and returned to her task.

She plucked handfuls of shiny, sugar-sweet tomatoes off of the vine and dropped them into her basket. She picked basil and rosemary from the little herb patch, and lifted a sprig to her nose.

She had almost filled up her basket when a strange sound startled her.

It was a *hissing* sound.

She looked around, but no one was there.

"Psst!"

She turned to look behind her, and almost screamed. The English reporter was *back* -- crouching in the bushes behind her!

"What are you doing here?" she cried, flushing in embarrassment. "And how long have you been hiding there!"

He stood up quickly, smiling. "I'm sorry, I'm not a stalker, I swear. It's just that this is the only way I could think of to talk to you again."

Jemima dropped the basket and began walking back toward the house. The man ran behind her.

"*Please,* don't run away – I'm not crazy, I'm a reporter. Look – here's my card!"

He hurried in front of her, and blocked her way.

She stopped dead, and her voice rose in panic. "If you don't leave me alone, *I'll call my father!*"

He was smiling, brows raised, his hands stretched out in a calming gesture. "There's no need for that! I'm going now. I just wanted to tell you that you need to get that letter appraised. It could be worth *hundreds of thousands of dollars.* I'm telling you, you might be rich! And I know where you can get it appraised. If you want to do it, I'll drive you there."

Jemima's eyes widened in terror. "I won't go anywhere with you!"

"My paper will *pay* to have the letter appraised. You don't even have to spend money, if you'll let me write a story about the letter. Just meet me back here on Monday, same time. I'll drive you to the appraiser's, and bring you back."

Jemima looked up into his face. His blue eyes were on fire with -- *something.*

His eyes flitted over her terrified expression, and he suddenly blurted: "I think you're the most beautiful woman I've ever seen in my life, and – and I don't even care about the letter, really. *Just let me see you again!*"

She screamed, picked up her skirts, and went flying towards the house.

He raised his eyes to the sky in despair, cursed himself,

skipped backwards a few paces and then began to run.

CHAPTER TWELVE

Jemima bounded up the steps to the back porch, ran inside, and fled up the back stairs and into her own bedroom. She slammed the door behind her and leaned against it, heart pounding.

She closed her eyes. She had *never* been so frightened in her life!

Her bedroom window overlooked the garden, and she inched over to peer out, though she was careful not to show herself. To her relief, there was now no sign of the intruder.

She frowned, thinking that her father had been right: the English were crazy, every one of them, and greedy for money.

She shuddered, remembering the look in that reporter's eyes: like they were on *fire* with insanity.

She rolled her own to the spot where she had hidden the

letter. That letter had caused her nothing but trouble since the day she had found it, even if it was sweet and touching, and possibly from George Washington.

Nothing was worth this much trouble.

She walked to the spot, and lifted the cover off of the hollow section. She grabbed the letter and took it in her hands, preparing to tear it into little pieces.

But the sound of her own name prevented her.

"Jemima!"

It was her mother calling.

"Jemima, you have a visitor!"

Her heart began pounding again, but this time with anger. She returned the letter to its hiding place, and opened the bedroom door.

If that crazy Englisher had come *inside the house*, she was going to call her father!

She ran swiftly downstairs, as outraged as she had ever been in her short life. But when she reached the living room, the person standing with her mother was only Samuel Kauffman.

Jemima's mother turned to her with a smile, but it soon faltered. "Why, Jemima, what's wrong? You look as if you…" her voice trailed off.

Jemima looked down at the floor, suddenly conscious that her face must be advertising her anger. "Nothing," she said quickly. "I was just – I was –"

"Samuel has paid us a call," her mother intervened quietly. "Why don't you talk with him, while I make some sandwiches?"

Jemima looked up at Samuel, and he smiled at her.

She nodded mutely.

"Let's go out to the porch," Samuel suggested. "It's cool out there."

Jemima followed him. He settled easily on the swing, and patted the seat beside him. She smiled, trying to focus her thoughts, and joined him.

They began to swing gently, back and forth.

Samuel had his hands clasped in his lap. He looked over at her, serious now.

"Jemima, I talked to your father the other day," he said quietly. "I asked for his permission to court with you. He was kind enough to give it."

He reached over and took her hand in his warm, brown one.

"But what do *you* say, Jemima?"

"I – I would say *yes,* Samuel, but –"

There was a sudden rustling in the bushes below the porch, and Jemima jumped as if she'd been shot.

"*What was that?*" she cried, and put a hand to her mouth.

Samuel frowned, and turned his head to look. "It's... one of your mother's chickens."

Jemima closed her eyes and leaned back against the swing. "*Oh.*"

He searched her face, and added: "Is something *wrong*, Jemima?"

Her eyes flew open, and met his earnestly. "Oh *no*, Samuel, nothing's wrong! I'm *happy,* I am, but --"

His expression cleared. "Then, it's all right with you, that we court?"

"Oh, yes, but, there's something –"

The sound of footsteps on the porch steps interrupted her. Mark and her father had returned to the house.

Jemima looked over at them in trepidation. Mark's eyes were glued to Samuel's, and were filled with outrage; her father's were on her own face, and were at first puzzled then worried.

Her father spoke first. "Jemima, is something wrong?"

Samuel spoke first. "No, sir, she was just startled by a chicken, or something."

Mark burst out, "Is that right, Jemima?"

She went beet red, and her father interjected, sternly, "That's for *me* to ask." He turned to her and raised his brows.

"There – there was something in the bushes, it was nothing," she stammered, in confusion, "everything is all right now."

"*All right?*" Mark echoed incredulously, and she looked at him pleadingly.

"You heard her!" Samuel answered, and stood up.

Jemima put a hand up, appealing to them both: "Don't be so quick to –" she began, but Mark took a step toward Samuel, and Samuel closed the gap between them.

Her father quickly pushed between them and said in an exasperated voice, "The *both* of you, go home. Now! You two hotheads aren't going to disrupt the peace of this house. And in the future, if either one of you wants to court with my daughter, you'll behave yourselves respectful -- or you won't be coming back!"

Mark and Samuel glared at one another then looked away.

"That's right! Now get gone -- before I lose my own temper!"

Mark shot Jemima a reproachful glance, and Samuel a warning one then stormed out.

Samuel turned to her, and extended a hand. "Don't let him upset you, Jemima," he said seriously. "May I come back again?"

She looked up, and nodded.

He smiled, and his blue eyes sparkled. "I'll be counting the days," he told her, in a low voice, and seemed ready to say more, but her father's hand on his shoulder made his straighten.

"*Now.*"

CHAPTER THIRTEEN

That night Jemima lay in her bed, staring at the ceiling, until well past midnight. The hum of crickets wafted in through her window, but so far had not been able to soothe her to sleep.

It had been a terrible day. She had been accosted by a crazy and frightening stranger, Mark and Samuel had shown up at the house on the same day -- and at the same *time*. Mark was mad at *her* for seeing Samuel, and now they were both angry at each *other*.

The two of them *had* been good friends. She turned her face into her pillow.

And what about that letter, still hidden in the wall nook? The reporter kept telling her that she might be rich, but she could honestly say that she didn't care. All she had *ever* wanted was to live in peace with a good Amish husband, near her family and friends. If that dream came true, she neither needed nor wanted anything else.

But clearly, the reporter did. *He wanted that letter.* That thing he had said about wanting to see *her,* about thinking she was *pretty,* she dismissed as a trick to get it.

A new thought came to her. What if she just – *gave* it to him?

Yes, she could just *give* it to him. Then he and everyone else who might want it would go away forever, and *leave her alone.*

Her spirits rose, only to be quenched by a new thought. *How would she get it to him?*

She tried to remember the name of the paper he said he worked for, but she couldn't.

She sighed. There was only one other alterative – to try to forget that the whole ugly incident ever happened, and to call her father if the English fellow ever showed his face to her again.

She sighed and nestled into the pillow. She had no doubt that her father would convince him to *mind his own business.*

The next morning was fair and clear and sunny. Jemima took up her basket, and resumed her usual chore in her mother's garden – gathering vegetables for the day's meal.

She hesitated to go to the same spot where the Englisher had ambushed her. She was reasonably certain that he wouldn't try a second time, but even so.

She ventured as far as the last row of pole beans, but only on the side nearest the house, so that if he was crazy enough to come back, she'd have a clear path back.

She scanned the bushes narrowly, but there was no sign of an intruder.

She picked fuzzy green bean pods and red peppers, and was about to move to the lettuce patch when something in her peripheral vision caught her eye.

She jumped, and rolled frightened eyes towards the house – but it was just a little spot of white lying on the grass.

She looked at the bushes again, and moved to take a closer look.

She bent down to pick it up. To her surprise – and relief – it was a business card. It read:

Brad Williams

Reporter, Ledger-Inquirer

bwilliams@ledger.com

There was also the phone number, and the newspaper's address.

Jemima breathed a silent prayer, and tucked the little piece of paper into her apron. Now that she had the man's address, she could mail the letter to him, and The Nightmare of the

English Letter would be over.

She turned back to the garden patch, and began humming.

That evening, when she had closed her bedroom door, Jemima sat down at a little table, took a sheet of paper, and began to write her letter.

Dear Mr. Williams, she began, *I do not want this letter, and I do not like people coming to my house without my permission because of it. If you want this letter, I will give it to you. I have no need to be rich, so you can be, if you want to be.*

Please do not come to my house again, or send anybody else.

Sincerely,

Jemima King

P.S. Or I will tell my father that you are there.

She folded the letter neatly. Then she picked up the old, yellowed letter and tucked it carefully inside the first one, and slid them both into an envelope.

She sat back in her chair and sighed in satisfaction. She would go to the post office and mail it the next morning.

She propped the letter on the table, turned down the lamp, and went to bed, where she slept soundly for the first time in days.

CHAPTER FOURTEEN

August bloomed fine and fair and hot, and though her mother's garden was in riotous bloom, heavy with melons and berries and ripening corn, Jemima was still no closer to a harvest in her own heart.

She still couldn't decide who she loved the most, out of so many. Mark and Samuel had redoubled their efforts, and shy, adorable Joseph Beiler was beginning to send her love letters.

"Jemima!"

Deborah came striding out to her, holding an envelope in her hands. "Here, Jemima," she said in a disgusted voice, "another page of *puke poetry* from Joseph Beiler."

"*Deborah!*" Jemima chided her, but her irritable younger sister was already on her way back to the house.

She looked down at the envelope. *Poor Joseph*, she thought sadly, as she tore it open. He *did* try, and it was the thought that counted, but no one was ever going to mistake him for a...

She opened the letter and was struck-staring in amazement.

The letter wasn't from Joseph Beiler at all.

It was from that Englisher, *Brad Williams!* She put a hand to her mouth and read the letter in shocked disbelief.

Dear Miss King, it read, *I have taken the liberty of showing your letter to a reputable appraiser, and he in turn has shared it with several experts on Revolutionary War documents. I have enclosed his report on the letter you sent me. I hope you will read it, because I think will please you to know the truth about your find.*

Jemima flipped the letter over. There was another letter beneath it, on very heavy, official-looking paper. The letterhead read: *Cheever and Cheever Appraisers, Philadelphia.*

Her eye skimmed quickly down the page.

Dear Ms. King, the letter read, *It is our great pleasure to inform you that the letter that was presented to us by Mr. Williams is, in our opinion, a genuine and previously unknown letter from George Washington to his wife, Martha.*

Jemima batted tears from her eyes, and hurried on.

It is well known that after George Washington's death, his wife burned his correspondence to her in an effort to preserve their privacy, and letters such as yours are, therefore, exceedingly rare.

While it is, of course, impossible to arrive at a precise value, since we consider the letter a priceless piece of Americana, we are willing to hazard a conservative estimate that it could bring a million dollars or more at auction.

Jemima went completely still. For a few long seconds, she could scarcely feel her own pulse.

If you should wish to put the letter up for sale, we would be happy to help you. At Mr. William's request, our bank is holding the letter for you in its vault for safekeeping, and it is available to you at any time.

Please advise us as how you wish us to proceed, and congratulations.

With warm regards,

Jonathan Cheever

The page fell back from her nerveless hand. She returned to the first letter, the one from Brad Williams. It read:

Thank you for offering to give me the letter, but as I told you earlier, my interest is in the story.

I would be very honored if you allowed me to tell this story for my paper, the Ledger. If you wish, I will not take any pictures of your face, or of your other family members. But I am convinced that our readership, and America at large, will be delighted by your good fortune, as I am myself.

Congratulations, and I hope to speak with you again. I have enclosed my number, if you would like to call. Should you choose to talk to me, I will be staying at Uncle Bob's Amish Motel for three weeks. You can send word to me there, if you like.

Cordially,

Brad Williams

Jemima dropped the letter and just stood there in the sunshine for several minutes. Then she looked up at the sky and spread out her hands in a wordless appeal.

She crushed the papers to her chest, bowed her head, and prayed hard.

Because she had the feeling that her life was never going to be the same.

THE END.

Thank you for Reading!

I hope you enjoyed reading this as much as I loved writing it! If so, there is a sample of the next book in the next chapter.

You can find the whole book in eBook and Paperback format at your favorite online book distributors.

Also, if you get a chance to give me a review, I would really appreciate it! Also, if you find something in the book you want to talk to me about (or YIKES -- something that makes you think it deserves less than 5-stars), please drop me a line at gr8godis76@gmail.com. I'll try to fix any problems if I can, and I love hearing from my readers in any case.

All the best,

Ruth

AN AMISH COUNTRY TREASURE 2

What happens when fun-loving Amish teen, Jemima King becomes an Amish Millionaire?

"Confidently written and genuine, Ruth Price gives us another unique, grounded, and utterly delightful Amish yarn!" - Rachel Stotlzfus, Amish Fiction Bestseller.

Seventeen-year-old Amish teen, Jemima King dreams of the blessings of marriage and family in her community, and with two rival Amish suitors pushing for a serious courtship, it seems like her largest problem will be choosing between them. But when a chance purchase puts Jemima in possession of a provocative national treasure, can she navigate the temptation of massive wealth and fame without losing what is truly precious? Find out in An Amish Country Treasure 2 by Ruth Price.

CHAPTER ONE

Jemima waited until night had fallen and the moon began its slow arc across the sky. When its smiling silver face appeared in the corner of her bedroom window, when the house had been quiet for hours, and when everyone else was asleep – she crept downstairs and out onto the front porch.

The moon was so bright that it cast shadows across the front yard, and the crickets hummed invisibly from the meadow.

Jemima sat down on the porch steps and looked out across the soft darkness, fragrant of mown grass and roses. She had always come to this spot as a child when she had been confused or upset because it was safe and quiet, and a good spot from which to watch the stars.

She looked up into the infinite night sky and questioned it with her eyes.

The George Washington letter was worth a million dollars – that was what the experts had said. And she'd been sure that once she'd given it to him, Brad Williams, the Englischer reporter, would've grabbed the letter and run. She'd been sure that he'd have sold it and gotten rich and never bothered her again.

But he hadn't done that.

She was still in shock.

Instead – unbelievably – he had thrown it right back into her lap.

Jemima had a fleeting suspicion that his gesture might still be some clever reporter's trick, but what could he hope to gain by giving the letter back – and giving up a fortune?

She had been taught to be wary of the Englisch, but what could she say when the Englisch fellow could simply have taken the million dollars – and yet chose instead to give it back to her? Who would ever have guessed that an Englischer could pass up the chance to be rich?

A strange tingling danced down her neck. What if the Englisch reporter really did mean what he said about wanting to see her again – for her own sake?

She pressed her brow against her arms. But of course, that was impossible, and would be wrong, anyway. He wasn't Amish, and so they had nothing in common.

Her thoughts returned to the thick, official-looking letters from the appraisers. They were a secret that she'd tucked away in the little hidden space behind her bedroom wall. She had told no one about them, not even her mother.

The ghost of a smile played across her lips. No matter what else happened, she was glad that the love letter itself had turned out to be real. It had been so sweet – so much the words of a man in love. Who would have thought it?

She wondered briefly if Martha Washington had been as

pierced by its beauty as she had been herself.

Wouldn't it be wonderful to have a husband who wrote you such letters?

She looked up at the sky, and just because there was no one there but her and God, and because there wasn't another soul awake within miles, she allowed herself to dream.

A tiny star trembled in the unfathomable distance and she watched it wistfully. If only there was a man who would tremble like that when she kissed him.

And who would tell her about his feelings so she didn't have to guess!

She closed her eyes. That was why the letter had been so beautiful. It had been written by a lover, not just a husband. A man who knew how to make himself vulnerable. A man who was strong enough to risk showing his heart without any attempt to protect it.

There were many boys who were willing to chase her, to kiss her, and do things for her. But not one of them, so far at least, had been willing to be naked in front of her – emotionally naked – and wasn't that what it truly meant to be intimate?

Wasn't love all about becoming vulnerable? Wasn't that…how you knew what it was?

That was what she dreamed of, at any rate: a man who was

strong enough to let love make him vulnerable. Who would open his heart and share his feelings. And none of the boys who were chasing her had made the faintest attempt. Clearly, that was because they didn't know that was what she really wanted.

But if she told them, then they'd all say what she wanted to hear, and she'd never know if it had been real or not.

Jemima opened her eyes. She knew that Mark and Samuel and Joseph were all capable of making themselves vulnerable to her. Maybe they were just too busy competing with each other to notice that she was looking for a man who knew how to lose his heart.

Not win a contest.

She sighed.

But, of course, that was just wishful thinking. Her mother had told her many times that romance was not the same as happiness, and Jemima knew that she was right. A man's integrity – his devotion to God and to his family – was what really made him a good husband.

And that was what made it so hard to choose between Mark and Samuel and Joseph. They were all good, they all had integrity, they all loved God and they would all be good providers.

And since they were all equally good, and all of them would likely make good husbands – would it be sinful of her to hope that she could find one who would make a good lover, as well?

Her mouth turned down gently. Not one, so far, had even told her that he loved her.

She had no doubt that all of them did – but they were Amish boys, and had been raised to show rather than tell.

Mark especially. She knew that he would do anything on earth for her, but he wasn't one to talk about it. Her lips curved, as she remembered all the ways he had shown her that he loved her: he never let her carry anything, he gave her candy and bites of his lunch and little gifts he had made with his hands – a carved wooden box, a tiny bird made out of copper wire, and pressed flowers. But Mark felt deeply, she knew.

And Samuel – he was far more likely to kiss her, than to murmur sweet nothings in her ear. But sometimes he looked at her with so much love in his eyes that it wasn't really necessary to hear the words. They were all there – right on his face. And when he took her hand, his touch was so tender and gentle that she would have had to have been a fool not to know that he loved her.

Joseph Beiler had big, melting brown eyes and thick dark hair and was as handsome as any movie star. But he was so shy that he was hardly able to string two words together in front of her – poor Joseph! Then he tried to make up for it by writing her poetry. She made a face, remembering his last effort: he had compared her to a beautiful cow. Her sister Deborah had been rude, but right: Joseph's heart was pure, but he was a terrible lover.

She looked up at the stars wistfully. Just now and then, it would be so nice to have a boy tell her what he felt when he looked at her. To let her see inside his heart.

And it wouldn't hurt at all, if he did it well.

Jemima brushed a tendril of hair out of her eyes. Her mother had told her many times that it was foolish to have your head turned by flowery words and pretty gestures.

"A good man shows love by what he does, Jemima," had been her teaching. "Not by what he says."

Jemima frowned. Her mother's wisdom had seemed so clear and right just a few days ago, and she knew that it was the truth. But even so, she was confused.

Because by that reasoning, her childhood friends and current suitors weren't the only ones who loved her. A strange Englisch reporter that she hardly knew had just shown her love.

Sort of.

And that made no sense at all.

CHAPTER TWO

Five o'clock came far too early the next morning, at least for Jemima King.

She dragged herself out of bed while it was still dark, dressed, and helped her mother cook breakfast; but she nodded over the stove as she cooked the eggs.

"Mind your hand, Jemima!" her mother cried sharply, and Jemima jerked her fingers back just in time to keep them from being burned on the hot metal. "Good heavens, child, you're sleepy! Didn't you get your rest?"

Jemima looked up at her apologetically. "No, I-I didn't get enough sleep last night," she confessed, blushing.

"Are you feeling all right?" her mother frowned, and put a hand to her cheek.

Jemima nodded, and the cloud lifted from her mother's brow. "Well, you must go to bed earlier tonight," she told her.

"Now help me set out breakfast. We can't be late for worship."

It was a Sunday morning, and worship was being held at the home of Aaron Kauffman, Samuel's father. It was on the far side of their church district, and it would therefore be necessary to get an early start.

Jemima set out a platter of sliced ham, and a bowl of biscuits, and fried potatoes. She was grateful when it came time to sit down, but she wondered how on earth she would ever stay awake through a two-hour sermon when she was starting out so tired.

Jacob King came walking in, stretching and yawning. "Good morning, my girls!" he told them, and leaned over to give their mother a peck on the cheek. "Ready for worship? It's a fine, fair morning, and not too hot. Are we set to eat?"

Rachel nodded, and sat down quickly. They all said a silent prayer, and then ate. Everyone but Jemima seemed to be in a good mood. Even Deborah wore a neutral expression through the meal, and for her that was as good as a smile.

But Jemima was worrying about the letter and chewed her thumbnail instead of her food. She could hardly concentrate on eating, wondering what on earth she was supposed to do now that she owned a document worth a million dollars. Nothing like that had ever happened to anyone she knew, or to anyone she had ever even heard about. What was she supposed to do now?

It felt sinful and greedy to keep such a thing. Surely such an important letter should be in a museum somewhere, not hidden away in a bank vault in her name.

But it would also feel sinful and greedy to sell it. A million dollars! What would an Amish girl like her even do with all that money? She already had all she needed, and it wasn't right to want more than that.

But, on the other hand, she had already tried to give it away, and to her total amazement that hadn't worked.

"Jemima!"

Jemima came to herself with a start. When she looked up, everyone at the table was staring at her.

"I-I'm sorry, I was-I was daydreaming," she stammered.

"About one of those silly pups, I suppose," her father replied, shaking his head. "Never mind, Mima! Just come along. It's time to get on the road."

Jemima followed them as they left. She climbed up into the buggy, and settled into the back seat, and watched the passing countryside without seeing it.

Maybe she should ask her parents what to do. But she dreaded the scolding they were sure to give her about talking to the Englisch reporter in the first place.

Then, too, if she told them what had happened, it would be the end of her own choice in the matter: they would forbid her to talk to any Englischer, ever again, as long as she lived.

And she would never find out if the Englisch reporter had meant what he'd said – or not.

She nibbled off another corner of her nail.

When they arrived at the Kauffman's home, she drifted alongside her family, nodding in response to greetings and keeping her eyes on the ground.

But soon Samuel appeared at her elbow, looking love at her out of those beautiful blue eyes.

"I missed you," he smiled, and a tender look was on his face. "Is your family staying for lunch, Jemima?" he asked in a lower voice. "I was hoping you and I could talk somewhere privately afterwards."

She looked up at him, and was about to answer, when her father noticed them. "Good morning, Samuel!" he said loudly. He clapped Samuel on the shoulder, pushed right in between them, and smiled broadly. "Beautiful morning, isn't it?"

"Yes, sir," Samuel replied, much less enthusiastically.

"And so much friendliness, everywhere I turn!" he added, shaking Samuel's shoulder. Samuel looked up at him with a chagrined expression.

"Jemima, go and find your mother and sister a place to sit and hold it for them," her father commanded, and she nodded submissively. She shot Samuel an apologetic look over her shoulder, and was grateful to see that his eyes were still fastened to hers.

But when she looked back again, just before entering the Kauffman's barn, she saw with a sinking heart that her father was talking earnestly to Samuel, and that her handsome blond admirer looked as though he'd been rained on.

She found a nice empty spot at the end of a bench, and waited for her mother and sister.

And sighed.

Soon her mother and Deborah arrived and settled in beside her, and the benches began to fill up. Jemima noticed Samuel took a seat just across from them on the front row of the men's benches. His eyes were on hers, and she smiled at him faintly. His eyes sparkled, and he winked at her – just once. It was over like lightning, and she doubted that anyone else even saw it. She lowered her head, to hide her laughter, but when she looked up again, she noticed that her father's eyes were on her and she assumed a more pious expression.

The service started with the singing of hymns, and after they were over, the sermon. The minister opened his Bible and began talking.

Jemima felt herself beginning to zone out. She was sleepy, she was confused about the letter, and she was distracted by Samuel. Because now and then, when she looked up, he would catch her eye. And do something silly.

Like flick his tongue out over his lower lip, like a snake. And she would have to lower her head again and try not to laugh.

Or roll his eyes up toward the ceiling, as if he were about to pass out. That time, she had to bite her lip to keep from laughing.

But eventually her father noticed where she was looking and gave Samuel such a freezing look that he had to stop playing.

The preacher talked and talked, and to Jemima it seemed that the sermon would never end. But at some point, after she had gotten quiet and had settled down, the words that the preacher was saying started to reach her.

He was talking about being a good Christian, and how that meant being kind to the poor. Jemima sighed and crossed her legs and looked through a window at the beautiful summer afternoon outside. She had heard this many times before.

But suddenly he raised his Bible in the air, and said:

"What if a miracle happened? What if I suddenly had a million dollars and yet kept it all for myself? What kind of a Christian would let a neighbor stay hungry? Or cold, or sick, if he had the power to help him?"

Jemima gasped, and rolled stricken eyes to the man's face. He was looking right at her.

"It's the duty of a Christian to do as Jesus would do," the man said earnestly. "And Jesus fed the hungry, and took care of the sick."

Jemima's eyes filled with quick tears.

"If we follow Jesus, we must do those things, too."

Jemima felt herself going hot. She lowered her face, to hide the tears in her eyes.

The man's words had pierced her heart like a sharp arrow. It was like God had spoken through him, straight to her.

She had prayed to God, asking Him what she should do with the letter. And she hadn't heard any answer.

Until now.

Now it was crystal clear. This, this was her answer: she was to sell the letter, and give the money to people who needed it.

It answered everything. She would not be selfishly hiding the letter away; she would not be greedily spending the money on herself. The money could be used to feed her hungry neighbors, and help those who were sick and needed medical help.

And that would even explain why the Englischer had given the letter back to her against all reason: it had plainly been the will of God – a miracle.

She lifted her eyes to the ceiling and put her palms up, in a gesture of pure gratitude to God. She mouthed silent words of worship, and smiled to herself.

And when she opened them again, she noticed that Samuel Kauffman was staring at her face. The silly look was gone.

His eyes were dead serious now. And the look in them was that of a man who would run through fire.

CHAPTER THREE

After the service, there was always a light lunch served inside the house and outside on the lawn. Jemima, like all the other girls, helped serve her elders until it was her own turn to dine.

It was a fine, clear morning with a blue sky and green grass and white tablecloths and people talking and laughing. Many of Jemima's elders greeted her pleasantly as she brought plates or pitchers to their tables.

Most of the boys stole shy glances at her face. She dimpled, and smiled at them, and watched in amusement as their faces went pink.

Afterwards, she joined her family and listened in dutiful silence as her father and their next-door neighbor talked crops. When she let her gaze wander, she noticed that Samuel was sitting at a table nearby. He was hard to miss when he took his hat off, his blond hair shone like corn silk against his black jacket. She noticed some of the other girls looking at him when he turned away, and she felt a little glow of gratitude. She was a lucky girl to have such a handsome young man pursuing her.

And he was pursuing her. It didn't take him long to sense her eyes on him. He smiled, and then got serious again and looked at her with such frank intent that she felt herself going hot. Samuel had beautiful blue eyes, and they expressed every feeling going through his heart as clearly as any sign.

She looked at him through her lashes. That was Samuel's charm – his glib laughter, and his carelessness, was all an act. He couldn't hide his true feelings – his eyes betrayed him every time.

And what his eyes were saying to her at the moment was probably best not said in a room full of people.

Jemima smiled faintly, well pleased, and dropped her own gaze demurely.

After everyone had eaten lunch, and she was free, Samuel appeared at her elbow. He whisked her away with him so quickly that even her father – who was talking to a neighbor about horseshoes – didn't have time to see them go.

Samuel took her hand and led her down a tortuous path that twisted crazily through a side door, down a few steps, through a narrow doorway, up a few stairs, and into a small sitting room in a hidden corner of their house.

Then he closed the door behind them and pulled her into his arms without another word.

Jemima went into them without a murmur and turned her face up to be kissed.

Samuel pulled her to his chest, twined his strong fingers in hers, pressed both hands behind her back, and kissed her with delicious tenderness. He was a delightful kisser – his lips seemed made for light, playful caresses, and he would pause mid-pucker sometimes, to pull back and look down at her until she opened her eyes. Then he would go on quirky kissing tangents, one kiss on each of her closed eyelids, lots of little kisses along her brows, and he might even plant a few stray kisses in the delicate, sensitive spot under her ear.

She giggled suddenly, and shook her head. "Oh, Samuel, that tickles," she laughed, turning her face away teasingly. "Didn't you shave your chin this morning?"

He looked down at her with a smile, and rubbed it with one brown hand. "Now that you mention it," he admitted ruefully, and his smile widened to a grin. "Tell me, does the scruffy look do anything for me?" He turned his profile, and she giggled again.

Then the smile faded from his lips. A serious look replaced them,

He pulled back, taking both her hands in his. "Jemima, I brought you here because I wanted to talk to you alone. I have something to say to you."

She held his gaze, waiting.

An uncharacteristic wave of shyness seemed to overwhelm him. "We-we've known each other a long time," he stammered.

"Yes, Samuel." She smiled, remembering the first time she had seen Samuel: he had been a mischievous little five-year-old boy making mud pies. He had looked up at her suddenly, his blue eyes and blond hair in stark contrast to a face covered in black mud. She had screamed and run away, and he had chased her.

He seemed to read the thought off her face. He relaxed a bit, and chuckled. "Yes, we go way back, don't we, Mima?" he said softly.

She looked up into his eyes and nodded, giving him her earnest attention.

"You know what kind of person I am, and I hope you feel about me, the same way I feel about you."

He massaged her hand gently, and half-smiled.

"After all – I asked to court with you, and you agreed."

Jemima's heartbeat quickened. She leaned in and looked deep into his beautiful eyes. Maybe Samuel was finally going to show her his heart. He might even tell her that he loved her.

And since he seemed to be shy, maybe she could help things along and give him a little nudge. Maybe she could gently remind him that there were other boys who might be willing to admit they loved her.

Maybe then he would confess his love, and pour out his heart, and make himself vulnerable – like in that magical letter.

She took a deep breath. "Yes, Samuel, we have been good friends. I agreed to see you. Not to see just you, but to go out. Just like you can see other girls, and not just me."

He raised his eyes to hers, and the look in them now was determined. Jemima's pulse quickened in anticipation. He was going to tell her he loved her at last. He was going to say it.

"I don't want to go out with any other girls, Jemima. And I don't want you to go out with any other men."

She held his eyes. "Why not, Samuel?" she asked gently.

Samuel looked pained. "Jemima, I-I–"

There was suddenly a thunder of pounding feet outside, and two little girls burst into the room, laughing and giggling.

"Abby, you're it!" shrieked a little pigtailed girl. "I caught you!"

"Count to ten!" the other one cried, and pressed herself against the wall. "One two three four…"

The pigtailed girl streaked out into the hall, only to collide with her outraged mother. "Ruth Beiler, stop that this instant! The noise you make – this isn't our house!"

She looked in and caught sight of the other child. "Abby Stoltzfus, is that you? Come out now, and stop this nonsense!"

The child obeyed in subdued silence, and the woman finally noticed Jemima and Samuel standing there. She looked embarrassed.

"Oh – I'm sorry," she murmured, and hustled the children out, but not before casting another curious, and frankly speculative glance at them.

After the door had closed behind the intruders, Samuel ran a hand through his rumpled blond hair, looked up at the ceiling, and then down at Jemima with a rueful sigh.

Jemima could have cried in frustration. There had been a confession trembling on Samuel's very lips, and it was slipping away – she could feel it. She pressed her hands against his chest.

"Oh Samuel, never mind them," she said earnestly, "you were going to tell me something. Don't hold back – I'm listening! Tell me now."

He smiled, gave a self-deprecating shrug, and cupped her cheek with his hand. "Mima," he said tenderly, "I–"

He leaned close. Jemima searched his eyes with her own,

but to her disappointment, no tender confession followed.

Unless she counted the gentle, softly rhythmic kiss that communicated so much.

And admitted exactly nothing.

CHAPTER FOUR

A week passed, in which Samuel called at the house again and used his handsome lips to kiss her much and confess little; Mark called at the house also, and also kissed her much, and told her even less; and Joseph mailed three regrettable pages of poetry in which he compared her to a large chicken, though she was fairly sure he was trying to say that she would make a good wife, in a very roundabout way.

She hadn't had much time to think about the letter, but the memory of it nagged at her. She had received what she believed to be direction from God to sell it, and the proper thing to do now was to call that Englisch reporter and get it over with.

But she dreaded it.

She counted it sheer Divine Intervention that he hadn't kept the letter for himself. That must surely be it, because she had no confidence in the fellow's ethics, or, to be honest, his sanity. He'd behaved like a madman the first day she met him. And his behavior hadn't improved – the last time she'd seen him, he'd jumped at her from the bushes in her mother's garden, like a wild animal.

He even pretended to be interested in her, though they were total strangers.

Still, it was her duty to sell the letter, and she supposed she'd better get on with it and have done. And since the crazy Englischer was the only person she knew that could help her, she guessed she ought to call him up.

Of course, it would all be very awkward, and not at all proper. As an Amish woman, she was not supposed to talk to Englischers and Englisch men in particular. But in a case like this, what other choice did she have?

She couldn't think of any other choice, anyway. But once the letter had been sold, and she had the money, no one would have to know what she'd done. She would just be an anonymous donor to people who needed help.

There was one possible problem, though: the Englisch reporter had said he wanted to write a story about her. That part did worry her. But since she didn't intend to see him again if she could help it, she supposed it would be all right to tell him her story over the phone.

There was little danger that her family and friends would ever find out. No one she knew read Englisch papers or visited their websites.

She sat on the porch swing, shelling beans into a big metal bowl. She still had the little card the reporter had given her. She could go out to the little phone shack at the end of their driveway and call. She would tell the Williams fellow to go ahead and put the letter up for auction.

Maybe she wouldn't even have to see him again at all. Maybe she could just tell him to take pictures of the letter, and tell him her story over the phone and tell him not to share her name.

Yes, that was it! She would give him permission to tell the story but not use her name. Then no one, not even the people who read the story, would ever know it was her.

Yes, that would be perfect. She smiled to herself, comforted by the belief that even if she had to do some unusual things at first, everything would be all right in the end.

Jemima put her plan into action early the next day.

At sunrise, she sat patiently on a small bench in the phone shack. The phone rang and rang…four times, five, six.

She wondered why the Englischer didn't answer his phone. He had written that he was staying at the motel outside of town. Surely he was up by now – it was almost 6 a.m., and the sky had been light for almost an hour.

After the tenth ring, there was a fumbling sound, and a clunk, and more fumbling. A bleary, irritable voice snapped:

"Very funny, Delores! Six o'clock in the morning! I'm reporting you to Dapper Dwayne for employee abuse. He'll be sending you a list of my grievances."

Jemima frowned. "I must have the wrong number," she stammered, and prepared to hang up the phone.

There was a frantic fumbling sound on the other end, followed by: "No, no, um, yes, this is Brad Williams. I'm sorry – is this – is this Miss Jemima King?"

Jemima frowned. He was babbling like a lunatic, and she was seized by the urge to hang up the phone and forget the whole thing. But the remembrance of the sermon she had heard spurred her to take a new grip on her resolve.

She took a deep breath. "Yes, it is."

"Ah! Ah, I apologize, Miss King. I, ah, mistook you for someone else."

She set her mouth, and replied firmly: "I'm giving you permission to sell the letter for me. You can give it to those people, and they can put it up for auction."

"Wonderful! I'd be delighted to help you! Would you be open to meeting me in town and letting me drive you out to the auction house?"

Jemima frowned into the receiver. His voice sounded

absurdly excited. She shook her head, thinking: Greed.

"I'm not going to meet with anybody," she told him firmly, "and I'm not going to the auction house, and I'm not going to get my picture taken. But if you want to ask me questions, I'll tell you about how I found the letter. But only if you don't use my name or my family's name."

"Ah." There was a split-second of silence, followed by: "I ah, appreciate that, Miss King! I would absolutely like to ask you questions about how you found the letter! Maybe I could come out to your house, it would only be for a–"

She shook her head vehemently. "No, I don't want anyone to come out to my house!"

"Okay, I understand," he replied quickly. "We can do it over the phone! I'll call you the day before the sale – when everything is ready."

"I'll call you," she told him.

"Or, you could call me," he amended quickly.

Jemima looked out the window toward the house. She only had a few minutes.

When she returned to the conversation, the reporter was saying, "Call me at this same number next Monday, about noon. I'll walk you through the small print, because there are some legal formalities. In order for us to sell the letter, you'll have to fill out some forms, and give the auction house your written permission to sell."

Jemima frowned. "Will they keep my name a secret?"

"If you want that."

Jemima nodded. "I do."

"I, ah, the appraisers recommended Brinkley's, is that all right with you?"

"Who's Brinkley?"

There was a long silence. "Ah…I'm sorry…Brinkley's is the auction house."

"As long as they keep my name private, and don't come out to the house or bother my family, I don't care who sells it," Jemima answered.

She looked up and saw her father standing on the front lawn with his hands on his hips. He was looking for her. Rufus was hitched to the buggy, and it was time to go back to Mr. Satterwhite's with the batch of dolls that she'd promised him.

"I have to go," she said suddenly. "I have to go to town."

"Wait – I mean, is it all right if I mail the documents to your home? You'll have to–"

But Jemima was no longer paying attention...

Thank you for Reading!

And thank you for supporting me as an independent author! I hope you enjoyed reading this book as much as I loved writing it! If so, you can find the rest of the book in eBook and Paperback format at your favorite online book distributors.

Also, if you get a chance to give me a review, I would really appreciate it! Also, if you find something in the book you want to talk to me about (or YIKES -- something that makes you think it deserves less than 5-stars), please drop me a line at gr8godis76@gmail.com. I'll try to fix any problems if I can, and I love hearing from my readers in any case.

All the best,

Ruth

ABOUT THE AUTHOR

Ruth Price is a Pennsylvania native and devoted mother of four. After her youngest set off for college, she decided it was time to pursue her childhood dream to become a fiction writer. Drawing inspiration from her faith, her husband and love of her life Harold, and deep interest in Amish culture that stemmed from a childhood summer spent with her family on a Lancaster farm, Ruth began to pen the stories that had always jabbered away in her mind. Ruth believes that art at its best channels a higher good, and while she doesn't always reach that ideal, she hopes that her readers are entertained and inspired by her stories.

CPSIA information can be obtained
at www.ICGtesting.com
Printed in the USA
LVHW081436060720
659893LV00035B/2534